To

From

W9-CJX-387

The Nutcracker

Adapted by Virginia Unser

Illustrated by Wendy Wallin Malinow
Designed by Lesley Ehlers

P P Peter Pauper Press, Inc.
White Plains, New York

Based on the 1816 story
Nutcracker and the King of Mice
by E. T. A. Hoffmann

For Caitlin Amber

Illustrations copyright © 1998
Wendy Wallin Malinow
Text copyright © 1998
Peter Pauper Press, Inc.
202 Mamaroneck Avenue
White Plains, NY 10601
All rights reserved
ISBN 0-88088-406-1
Printed in China
14 13 12 11 10 9 8

Visit us at www.peterpauper.com

Christmas Eve

A great whirl of snowflakes and wintry wind blew open the carved doors, spilling velvet-clad guests into the warmth of the Stahlbaums' entrance hall. At last, it was time for the Christmas party!

Five-year-old Marie could scarcely contain her excitement. After weeks of preparation, Christmas had finally arrived! Mama and Papa swept through the hall, greeting family members, as the guests shook snow from their furs. Children scampered around the adults. The little boys ran off to the parlor to drill their toy soldiers. Wooden sword in hand, Marie's elder brother Fritz led the band of boys with a war-cry.

The little girls clustered around Marie, who proudly displayed her new doll, christened "Clara." All the girls agreed that she was the loveliest doll they'd ever seen, with curling tendrils of golden hair and eyes of the clearest azure. In fact, Clara bore an astonishing resemblance to little Marie.

Primping and cooing, the circle of young ladies drifted in the direction of the children's parlor. A fierce battle raged there, punctuated by the boys' shouts and the *pop!* of cannon-fire. Soldiers lay strewn across the carpet, and, as the girls tried daintily to sidestep them, the boys charged forward, en masse, to give chase.

"Here! Here!" shouted Fritz, waving his sword, "I am the Great Mouse King! Catch me if you can!" The other boys followed, shrieking horribly, in pursuit of the girls who scattered in all directions, screaming at the tops of their voices.

The children streamed into the drawing room, where their parents, aunts, and uncles had just finished dressing the grandest of Christmas trees. Its majestic boughs beckoned and bobbed with gold and silver globes. Tiny carved figurines sparkled with gilt paint, and all kinds of sugared fruits dangled enticingly just out of reach. Glass clowns twinkled amongst real gingerbread and exotic birds fashioned from feathers and gems.

Little toys and sweets hung from the branches where the children could pick them. Gracefully, the branches tapered upward, culminating in a glittering spire. At the end of each slender bough sat a candle. The tree came alive with thousands of dancing lights, each a prismatic angel.

The children stopped, transfixed. "Oh, Mama! Papa!" cried Marie as the great doors flew open with a whoosh! A draft of frosty air spilled in as a figure stepped into the sanctuary of the hall.

Fully six feet tall, this man was dressed in a cloak of richest purple, which reached all the way to his brass-buckled shoes. The hem of his cloak was decorated with the most elaborate gold braid, and epaulets rested upon his shoulders. Atop his head sat a towering tricorn hat, emblazoned with the golden figure of an eagle.

The man wore a black patch over one eye, while with the other bright blue eye he regarded the assembly calculatingly along the length of his patrician nose. Under one arm he carried a large, irregularly shaped package wrapped in sparkling paper.

In unison, the children shouted, "Uncle Drosselmeier!"

Everyone began talking at once as adults and children alike crowded around the strange visitor.

"Uncle Drosselmeier, I do hope you've brought a cavalry for me," Fritz began, tugging at the purple cloak.

"What about me?" called one child, "And what about me?"

called another.

Marie stood back as the other children chattered excitedly around Drosselmeier. He withdrew an oversized pocket watch hanging on a chain, and consulted it, while rubbing his chin.

"All in good time, my boy. Never forget that your Uncle Drosselmeier the clockmaker does everything by the clock!"

Then he looked up. His good eye lighted on Marie, and a smile crinkled the corners of his eyes.

"My dearest niece," he said softly. Marie smiled and twirled, letting her party dress spin around her. She hugged her uncle.

"It's so good to see you, Uncle Drosselmeier!"

The children still swarmed about Drosselmeier as he entered the drawing room and seated himself upon a chair in the center of the room. He placed his box on the floor and opened the lid.

From this ingenious box, he brought forth dozens of toys and novelties, several for each child. Fritz did indeed acquire his cavalry, mounted on splendid steeds. The other boys received tin horns, drums, caps, and swords, while Uncle Drosselmeier gave the little girls hair ribbons, lockets, and cunning toy animals. Each of the children was given a puzzle and a picture book.

Reaching both hands into the box, Drosselmeier lifted out a pirouetting ballerina almost as tall as Marie herself. She balanced on one toe on the floor and spun round in a tutu that looked as though it had been fashioned from clouds and snowflakes. Another dancer, a prince dressed in crisp blue, joined the ballerina, and they performed a *pas de deux* for the guests.

Still, Marie stood away from the other children, watching solemnly as the treats were passed out. At last Drosselmeier appeared to reach the bottom of his magical box. The twirling mechanical dancers slowed and stopped, crimson smiles fixed upon their unseeing faces. The children began to wander away, examining and comparing their treasures.

Again Drosselmeier fixed his gaze on Marie. He crooked a bony finger at her and she stepped forward. The rest of the room, the dancing adults, the chortling children, seemed to recede, until she felt quite alone with her uncle. The intensity of his stare made her feel that he could see into her very soul.

Drosselmeier whispered, "I have brought a most extraordinary gift for my precious niece. All is not what it seems!" Bewildered by Drosselmeier's words, Marie looked up at her uncle. What

could he mean? Before she could ask him to explain, Drosselmeier reached into the box and handed something to Marie.

She held in her arms a wooden man. Marie moved each of his body parts—head, arms, legs—and found that he was quite mobile. She examined her gift.

This unusual little wooden figure possessed a body that was too tall and fat for his legs, which were short and skinny, and his head was much too large for his body. The elegance of his costume, however, made up for a great deal. It showed him to be a person of taste and cultivation. He was wearing a purple military jacket with knobs and braid all over, pantaloons of the same purple as the jacket, and the finest boots ever seen on an officer—boots which fit his little legs as if they had been painted on. It was strange, however, that for all this fine style he wore over his shoulders a rather ridiculous short cloak that looked almost as if it were made of wood, and on his head a cap like a miner's. Marie looked at the little man, then at Drosselmeier, and then back again. The likeness was remarkable.

Marie fell in love with this little man at first sight. She gazed into his face and saw clearly that he had a very sweet personality. His blue eyes (which stuck, perhaps, a little farther out of his head than was quite desirable) beamed up at her with kindness and good cheer. His chin was set off with a tidy beard of white cotton, which was another of his good features. This beard drew attention to the smile that was always on his bright red lips.

"Oh, Uncle Drosselmeier!" Marie twirled around with delight.

"Please allow me the pleasure of introducing to you my dear friend, Nutcracker," Drosselmeier said with great drama. Marie curtsied deeply. Drosselmeier took her little hand and placed it to Nutcracker's lips.

"Enchanted."

Marie was sure that she could feel warmth and pressure where her hand had touched Nutcracker's rosy mouth. But she scarcely had time to ponder this inexplicable point before Drosselmeier had summoned the children back to the drawing room. He took a walnut out of his case and placed it between Nutcracker's jaws. Lifting the sword that hung by Nutcracker's side, he brought it down slowly.

C-rack!

The shelled walnut fell into his hand in two pieces. He

handed the nut to Marie, who ate it.

"Oh, please, another!"

The children clustered around Marie and the ingenious contraption. Everyone clamored for a turn. For several minutes, Nutcracker was put through his paces, cracking nuts as fast as his jaws would allow.

"Perhaps," Uncle Drosselmeier said, as the children continued to marvel at Nutcracker, "you would be interested to hear how Nutcracker came upon his unusual appearance and occupation."

"Yes, please!" the children chimed.

One by one, the children plopped onto the floor by Drosselmeier's feet, where Marie sat, cradling Nutcracker on her lap.

The Princess Pirlipat, Uncle Drosselmeier began, was born to a king and queen in a faraway land. Her birth was occasion for great rejoicing. Everyone agreed that there had never been a lovelier baby than Princess Pirlipat.

All was joy and gladness except for one thing. The queen was very anxious and uneasy, though nobody could tell why. She insisted that Pirlipat's cradle be very carefully guarded. Not only did she keep soldiers at the nursery doors, but she also stationed nurses next to the cradle. But what seemed strangest of all was that these nurses were required to have cats on their laps and to pet them all night long, so that they would never stop purring.

Dear children, let me explain how all these strange precautions came about.

Once upon a time, many powerful kings and queens assembled at the court of Pirlipat's father. To entertain these great nobles, he decided to dip into the royal coffers and give a grand sausage banquet. After having checked with both the master chef and the court astronomer to find an hour appropriate for sausage-making, he proceeded to invite guests from realms near and far.

Having done this, he drew his faithful queen aside and said, "My darling, only you know exactly how I like my sausages!"

The queen understood that this meant that she would have to prepare the sausages herself. She ordered the chancellor of the treasury to take the great golden sausage kettle out of storage.

While the queen worked, she suddenly heard a delicate whisper: "Psst, lady! Give me some sausage! I'm a queen just like you!"

It was the Mouse Queen, Dame Mouserinks, who had

resided in the palace for many years. She was the queen of the realm of Mousolia, where she lived with a considerable court of her own under the kitchen hearth.

Pirlipat's mother was a kind-hearted woman. She said, "Come out, Dame Mouserinks. Of course you can taste my sausages."

Dame Mouserinks ran out as fast as she could, and took one morsel of sausage after another as quickly as the queen held them out.

Soon all Dame Mouserinks' uncles and cousins and aunts scurried into the kitchen, all demanding their share of sausage, and the queen did not dare refuse them, until the mice had devoured every bit of sausage in the kingdom.

The next evening, the guests gathered for the feast. As they waited for the sausages to be served, the queen entered the banquet hall and whispered something in the king's ear. The king turned pale and raised his eyes heavenward. Clearly a terrible pain assaulted him. Finally he fell back in his seat, groaning and wailing.

He stammered, "No sausages!"

The queen threw herself at his feet, and cried, "Dame Mouserinks and all her family came and gobbled up the sausages—"

The king swore to take revenge on Dame Mouserinks and her family for devouring the sausages. Then he called in the court clockmaker whose name was the same as mine—Christian Elias Drosselmeier.

The clockmaker promised that he would rid the palace of mice once and for all. He invented very small and clever mouse-traps, into which pieces of cheese were inserted. Mouserinks herself was much too smart to be taken in by Drosselmeier's scheme, but her efforts to warn her relatives of the danger were useless. Lured by the tantalizing smell of cheese, her entire family was soon taken prisoner and put to death. The Mouse Queen was able to save only herself and her son, whom she hid away in the root cellar, far from Drosselmeier's traps.

One day, Dame Mouserinks appeared before the queen and said, "Beware, lady . . . for I will avenge the deaths of my family!"

Fritz interrupted, "Tell us, Uncle Drosselmeier, was it really you who invented the mousetraps?"

Drosselmeier laughed and said, "Well, don't you think I'm a

good clockmaker—and shouldn't a good clockmaker know how to make a good mousetrap? Now then, as I was saying . . . " Drosselmeier resumed his story.

"Now you understand, children," said Drosselmeier, "why it was that the queen took such measures to guard her precious little Pirlipat. She was constantly afraid that Dame Mouserinks would bite the little princess!"

One night, one of the nurses stationed near the cradle woke from a nap. Suddenly this nurse saw, right before her eyes, a huge, hideous mouse, standing in the baby's cradle! Everybody woke up at the shriek. But Dame Mouserinks ran off and away, through a crack in the floor. The noise awoke Pirlipat, and she gave a miserable wail, or, more accurately, a pitiful squeak. To everyone's horror, Mouserinks had transformed the baby girl into a baby mouse, complete with little gray ears, black button eyes, whiskers, and a pink tail!

Of course, the queen nearly died of weeping and lamentation. The king laid the blame on the court clockmaker, Christian Elias Drosselmeier, and drafted a decree stating that Drosselmeier must restore Pirlipat to her original condition, or be beheaded.

Not knowing what to do, Drosselmeier began to weep bitterly while little Princess Pirlipat kept herself happy by cracking nuts. He was suddenly struck by Pirlipat's remarkable appetite for nuts. Immediately after her transformation by Dame Mouserinks, she had gone on crying until by chance she was given a nut. After cracking it open and eating the kernel, she became quite peaceful. From that moment on, her attendants were never able to bring enough nuts to satisfy her.

"The mystery is solved!" shouted Drosselmeier. He immediately sought out the court astrologer. Together they consulted the stars and drew up the princess's horoscope. At last—hurrah!—it was clear: to break the spell, Princess Pirlipat had to nibble on the kernel of the sweet nut Krakatuk.

Now, Krakatuk had such a hard shell that you could have fired a forty-eight pound cannonball at it without cracking it in the slightest. Nonetheless, for the spell to be broken, this hard nut would have to be broken between the teeth of a man who had never shaved, and who had never worn boots. Furthermore, he would have to hand the kernel to the princess, and then take seven steps backwards without stumbling—with his eyes closed.

Drosselmeier and the court astrologer traveled for fifteen years without finding any trace of the nut Krakatuk. They nearly gave up hope. Dejectedly, they returned to the palace, sure that they would lose their heads. On the way there, they paid a visit to Drosselmeier's cousin, the dollmaker, Christoph Zacharias Drosselmeier, whom Drosselmeier hadn't seen in many years. The clockmaker poured out his tale of woe to his cousin.

"Cousin, cousin! I have the nut Krakatuk myself!" said Christoph.

Wasting no time, he brought out a little cardboard box, from which he took a gilded nut. Any doubt as to whether his cousin's nut was the long-sought Krakatuk vanished in a moment, when Drosselmeier carefully scraped away the gilding and found the word Krakatuk engraved on the shell in Chinese characters.

As Drosselmeier and the astrologer congratulated themselves on their good fortune, the astrologer observed, "I believe we've found not only the nut, but also the young man who will crack it and hand the kernel to the princess! I mean none other than the son of your cousin!"

Cousin Christoph Zacharias's son was, in fact, a good-looking, well-formed young man who hadn't yet shaved and had never worn boots. He would stand proudly in his father's shop and, with natural gallantry, crack nuts for the young ladies, who called him "the handsome nutcracker."

The trio hurried at once to the palace.

Young Drosselmeier, after he had bowed to the king, the queen and to Princess Pirlipat, placed the nut Krakatuk between his teeth and *k-nack-k-nack!* the shell shattered into countless pieces. He then neatly cleaned away the pieces of husk that were sticking to the kernel and, with a polite flourish, he presented it to the princess. As soon as she took it, young Drosselmeier closed his eyes and began to walk backward.

The princess instantly swallowed the kernel, and—what joy it was to see!—the girl was transformed. Gone were the mousy ears, the gray fur. There stood before the court an angelically beautiful girl with a face that seemed woven of delicate lily-white and rose-red silk, with eyes of sparkling azure, and hair like curling threads of gold.

The blare of trumpets and kettledrums mingled with the people's loud rejoicing. The king and his entire court danced around on one leg, and the queen had to be revived with Eau de Cologne, as she had fainted from joy and delight.

The uproar threw young Drosselmeier off balance—remember, he still had to finish taking his seven backward steps. But he controlled himself as best he could. Then—hideously peeping and squeaking—up came Dame Mouserinks through the floor. As young Drosselmeier put his foot down, he couldn't help stepping on her, and he stumbled and almost fell.

With her dying breaths, Dame Mouserinks squeaked a terrible prophecy:

"Beware, take heed, nut-cracking foe!
Soon you as well to death will go!
My son's seven-headed crown
Will seek you out and bring you down!
Crack nuts, you will, forevermore,
Until true love your looks restore!"

The horror of it! All at once the youth was transformed. His head grew larger, and he now had enormous popping eyes and a wide gaping mouth. Where the handsome young suitor had stood, there now stood a wooden Nutcracker.

"Eeeek! Somebody take away that awful Nutcracker!" shrieked Princess Pirlipat.

The King seized Nutcracker and his uncle and threw them out the door, banishing them from the kingdom forever.

"That, my dear children," said Drosselmeier, "is the story of the hard nut. Now you know why people so often use the expression 'that was a hard nut to crack,' and why nutcrackers are so ugly. And that ends the tale!"

Marie thought Princess Pirlipat was a vile and ungrateful thing. Fritz, however, felt that if Nutcracker really were the right kind of fellow, he would soon bring the Mouse King into line and win back his good looks.

Drosselmeier rose, and gathered his belongings. He shook Fritz's hand firmly and then each of the boys' in turn. He gave the little girls a pat on the head, until he came, last, to Marie. He raised her small hand to his lips, as the Nutcracker had done. Once again, Marie felt as though she moved in a dream.

"Be faithful and true, dear Marie," he said.

In a flurry of good wishes and swishing of ladies' skirts, Uncle Drosselmeier departed into the snowy evening. Marie stared out the window at the lacy flakes for several minutes, still clutching Nutcracker. Her mother took her hand and led her away from the drafty window.

Marie asked, "Mama, please may I look after Nutcracker tonight? He can sleep in my doll's house."

"Nonsense, Marie!" Fritz shouted, "Nutcracker's a fighting fellow! He'll bunk with my men in the barracks."

"You weren't the least interested in him until Uncle Drosselmeier told that story," said Marie, grabbing Nutcracker, "He needs his rest if he's going to chase off that horrible mouse king."

"He's a soldier, I tell you!" Fritz tried to wrest Nutcracker from Marie's grasp. "Come, Papa! Watch what he can do!"

The other children, and some of the adults, gathered around when they observed the ingenious device being demonstrated once more. The children pawed at Nutcracker, jostling one another for a turn. Fritz stepped back from the others and snatched the biggest, hardest hickory nut from a bowl on the table and wedged it in Nutcracker's mouth. He brought the sword aloft.

"Stop it!" Marie could hardly bear to watch.

They struggled for a few moments, each of them hanging onto one of Nutcracker's arms. With all his strength, Fritz pulled hard on Nutcracker's sword.

Snap!

Out came the hickory nut, shelled and ready to eat. Out, too, came three of Nutcracker's teeth. They dropped onto the floor, leaving poor Nutcracker with a jagged smile and a wobbly jaw.

"Look what you've done," she sobbed, "Mama, look at what Fritz has done!"

"Children, that's quite enough," Father said, picking up Nutcracker's broken teeth, "I can assure you that Uncle Drosselmeier will not be pleased by this turn of events!"

Ashamed, Fritz and Marie hung their heads. The other children stared at their shoes. Mama dried Marie's tears with her handkerchief. "I think we've all had far too much Christmas excitement, and our heads stuffed too full with Uncle Drosselmeier's tales. What we all need is a good night's sleep. We'll fix up Nutcracker in the morning."

Father bound Nutcracker's broken jaw stoutly with a piece of bandage cloth and placed him gently on a shelf in the glass-fronted cabinet. Marie perched on a stool near the door, keeping watch over her new friend.

The adult guests soon collected their children and wrapped them in furs for the trip back home. The Stahlbaums said goodbye to their relations. Mama snuffed out the candles one at a time, leaving just one lamp burning in the drawing room. In the soft light, the Christmas tree appeared even grander than it had before.

"Come, Marie, darling," Mama said.

Reluctantly, Marie waved goodbye to Nutcracker.

Fritz and Marie submitted to being dressed in their night-clothes and tucked in their beds. After Mama blew out the candle, however, Marie found herself unable to close her eyes. She heard skittering and scratching in the walls, above her head—everywhere! Could it be . . . the rustling of tiny mouse-feet? Could the Mouse King be here, in this very house? She pulled the covers over her head, but the sounds increased, until they became a deafening din punctuated by squeaks and high-pitched shouts. She thought of poor Nutcracker, lying all alone and cold downstairs. She had to protect him!

Icy and trembling with fear, Marie crept out of her bed and

slipped her feet into her velvet slippers. Edging along the wall, Marie padded down the staircase, toward the source of the noise, which emanated from the drawing room. Now devoid of party guests, the glossy wooden floor stretched on endlessly. Squares of moonlight reflected silver, and gave play to shadows and phantoms. Bare branches tap-tapped against the window panes as the wind rattled the eaves. In the course of the evening's excitement, Fritz had neglected to put away his soldiers, and they still lay where they had fallen on the floor. Tiptoeing past them, Marie hid in a corner and watched with her fingers in her ears.

She looked across at the great grandfather clock. The hands stood precisely upright, pointing to midnight. Then she spied a figure standing on top of the clock—a figure with white hair and a black patch over his eye. He wore a coat with long tails, which he spread across the face of the clock.

"Uncle Drosselmeier!" whispered Marie, "What are you doing here?"

He had no chance to reply, for the clock struck solemnly: *Bong! Bong!* exactly twelve times.

Marie felt small and helpless. Chill gusts swept past her,

swirling the draperies into fantastical shapes. It seemed that every object in the room was expanding, growing bigger and more menacing.

Once so benign and welcoming, the Christmas tree appeared to enlarge, until its majesty towered over the scene. Thousands of white lights blazed in its mighty branches, and the decorations swayed in the sudden wind. The gingerbread men began to twitch, and the clowns to titter.

The roar grew even louder. Then, to Marie's astonishment, row upon row of mice marched in precise formation from the fireplace, across the hearth, and toward the magnificent Christmas tree. At the head of their ranks strode a huge creature in full military regalia. Golden epaulets bristled upon his shoulders (he walked on two legs), and a bandolier studded with bright brass ammunition glittered across his barrel chest. He wore white breeches and atop his head sat a fantastic crown consisting of seven mouse-heads with bejeweled eyes that appeared to be looking everywhere at once. Each one of these seven hideous heads wore its own gold crown, a miniature version of the original.

This mouse's wiry pink tail curled behind him, alert. A terrifyingly sharp scimitar hung at his side. He glanced neither to the

right nor to the left, and his long yellow teeth and red eyes gave him a horrific appearance. Marie knew at once that he was the Mouse King himself.

His minions followed him, also in breeches, shiny boots and blue coats. Each carried a sword. The glitter of scores of eyes was truly ghastly to behold.

Marie shrank into the corner as the ranks of the Mouse King marched ever closer to her beloved Nutcracker. She could feel those eyes peering at her from every crevice!

Then another magical thing happened. One by one, Fritz's dragoons and swordsmen—along with his shiny new soldiers—marched out and lined up on the floor. They trooped past in regiments, banners flying and bands playing. After this maneuver, they wheeled and formed up at right angles to the line of the march, while Fritz's artillery came rolling into position at the front.

Fritz's Italian clown Pantaloon leaped across the floor to lead the troops, shouting,

"Wake up! Wake up! It's time to fight!
The battle starts this very night!
Wake up, wake up—and fight! And fight!"

At once, the cannons commenced to fire. *Boom! Boom! Boom!* Marie saw sugarplum ammunition wreaking havoc among the thickly massed mouse battalions, covering them with white sugar-powder. A division of heavy guns, which had taken a strong position on Mama's footstool, did the greatest work. *Bam! Bam! Bam!* They kept up a murderous fire of gingerbread nuts on the enemy's ranks, mowing the mice down in dozens.

Toys of all sorts ran about, struggling with toy weapons. Two dolls pushed a cannon to the front of the ranks. A stuffed poodle nudged along the jack-in-the-box, while the farmyard animals set up a dreadful squawking.

The mice charged forward, baring their teeth. The wooden soldiers suffered awful bites, but Fritz's lead and tin troops were able to hold off the rodent horde for a short while. Indeed, when the mice tried to bite them, their teeth clanked and cracked, frightening the mice, who then rushed, squealing mightily, back into their own lines, creating chaos.

Swords clashed! Metal rang on metal; sparks flew as the courageous soldiers held the line, sometimes fighting hand-to-hand with their foes.

At once, a noble figure appeared, splendidly dressed in a purple coat, his dazzling sword drawn. It was Nutcracker!

"My trusty friends and followers!" he shouted, springing to the head of the troops. "Stand fast and victory will be ours! Sound the clarion!"

The buglers blew with all their might; the drummers drummed fiercely. Again and again the cannons fired! *Boom! Boom!*

The infantry rushed into the fray, straight at the front ranks of the mouse army. Oh, the fighting was terrible! Nutcracker slashed away at the mice, inflicting grave damage. The screeches of the fallen mice raised a bloodcurdling din as Nutcracker surged forward.

Alas, the brave soldiers were no match for the savagery of the mice. For every mouse that fell in the battle, two rose to take his place. Their shrieks filled the air, and Nutcracker's army suffered heavy casualties. Old and soft, Pantaloon was unable to hold his position in front of the cabinet, and a squadron of mice seized his artillery. With gleeful squeaks, they turned the cannon on the soldiers, scattering them willy-nilly across the battlefield. Sensing weakness, the Mouse King sped over and delivered a brutal bite to the clown, spilling his sawdust stuffing onto the floor.

"Oh, woe! I am fallen!" Pantaloon cried, clutching his side.

Marie's dolls wept and lamented, sure that they, too, would perish or be taken prisoner.

"Save us! Oh, Nutcracker! Please save us!" They cowered near Marie, who tried to shield them with her dressing gown.

Nutcracker sprang to the aid of his comrade. Cold fire flashed in his blue eyes. Slowly, the Mouse King turned his bloated body to face his enemy. His crimson eyes glittered with rage. He drew his sword from its scabbard with an ear-splitting scrape. Nutcracker unsheathed his in turn. The blades glinted in the moonlight. Marie held her breath.

"At last, we meet on the field of battle, Nutcracker! Prepare to die! I'll avenge my mother's death with Nutcracker's dying breath! Qweek!"

The Mouse King leapt with agility surprising for one so large, but Nutcracker was quicker and feinted. *Clang! Clang!* Their swords crashed against each other over and over.

Nutcracker yielded a step, and then another. Marie could see beads of perspiration forming under his plumed hat. The Mouse King deflected his blows easily. A few more steps backward, and Nutcracker was trapped between the cabinet and the Christmas tree. The mouse army began to close ranks around their leader. Still, Nutcracker fought on, slashing this way and that, his sword like lightning.

But Marie knew that Nutcracker would soon tire under such an onslaught. How could he hold out against such numberless enemy? His arm slowed, and he did not raise it so high as he had at the beginning of the battle.

"Oh, no!" thought Marie. "I've got to do something to help Nutcracker!"

Almost without thinking, she removed her slipper and flung it as hard as she could into the thick of the enemy—straight at the Mouse King!

Instead of hitting the evil creature, however, Marie's slipper struck one of the pendulous ornaments dangling from the Christmas tree: a silver orb. It shattered into thousands of shards, momentarily stunning the Mouse King and his troops.

Nutcracker wasted no time going straight for his mark. He lunged forward, driving his blade deep into his foe.

The Mouse King lurched and staggered. In a panic, mice

raced in all directions. When their leader fell dead with a *thud!* they squeaked with fright, and scrambled over one another in their haste to escape a similar fate. The soldiers brandished their weapons and chased the enemy to the far corners of the room, where the mice finally disappeared, banished forever.

A moment of silence descended upon the battlefield. Marie, who had hidden her face at the last moment, finally remembered to draw a breath, and she slowly looked up.

Splinters of glass lay everywhere on the floor. Toy soldiers were piled higgledy-piggledy, and little silver musket-balls were scattered about. Moreover, Marie suddenly became aware that she and the toy figures were equal in height. She did not think it at all unusual that the drawing room furniture now towered above them.

Alas, the Mouse King had fallen right on Nutcracker! Marie scrambled across the debris and pushed the evil king off her savior.

"Nutcracker! Oh, my poor, brave Nutcracker! Please tell me that you're unharmed!" She leaned over and kissed Nutcracker's lips, which felt soft and warm. His eyelids fluttered open, and he smiled when he saw Marie.

"Yes, dear Marie . . . I have escaped injury, thanks to you!

Oh, gracious lady," he said, rising to one knee and sheathing his sword, "I owe my life to you."

Marie's eyes widened, for Nutcracker had been transformed! Where the odd Nutcracker had been, there now stood a very handsome young gentleman, of rosy complexion and the bluest of eyes. He wore an elegant red coat trimmed in gold, with white silk stockings and shoes, and a lovely nosegay in his short frill. The sword at his side sparkled and shone—it seemed to be made entirely of jewels.

He continued, "It was you, and only you, dearest lady, who inspired me with courage. Now the wicked King of Mice has perished. Please consent, dear Marie, to accept these tokens of victory from the hand of the one who is your true and faithful knight. Behold, how your valor and loyalty have broken the spell of Dame Mouserinks! No longer am I a lowly Nutcracker!"

Pantaloon rose stiffly, with one hand over the wound in his side. He bowed before Nutcracker, the feathers of his cap brushing the ground.

"Hail, Nutcracker! You have seized the victory from the jaws of evil! Bravo!"

A cheer went up amongst the soldiers, some of whom tossed

their hats in the air.

"Hip, hip, hooray for Nutcracker!"

Smiling, Nutcracker acknowledged the accolades of his troops with a salute. He strode forward until he stood a few steps from Marie. He took the seven-headed crown of the Mouse King from his left arm and presented it to her.

Remembering her manners, Marie curtsied and accepted the crown. She suddenly felt shy, and a flush had crept into her cheeks, which had been so very pale with fright during the thick of the battle. Then she heard a sound like a little bell singing, "Marie so fine—oh angel mine! I will be thine, if thou wilt be mine! Now that I have finally defeated my longtime enemy, I can show you such wonderful things! If you would just be so good as to follow me for a few steps."

Nutcracker extended his arm, and Marie took his hand. Together they stepped into the patch of moonlight, and the wind blew open the French doors. As the curtains parted, Marie glimpsed a new, wonderful world.

Marie stepped out into a snowy forest. Icicles dripped from the fir trees. When Marie touched one, she discovered that it was

not made of ice at all, but of crystalline sugar candy!

"How wonderful this is!" Marie said, enraptured.

"This is Christmas Forest," said Nutcracker, clapping his hands.

Immediately there arrived a troupe of shepherds and shepherdesses, as well as hunters and huntresses, all of whom were so white and delicate that you would have thought they were made of pure sugar. They carried with them a white satin chair, and courteously invited Marie to take a seat. As soon as she did so, the shepherds and shepherdesses performed a pretty ballet before her, while the hunters and huntresses played music upon their horns.

As the music swelled, snowflakes drifted down from the heavens, filling the air with thousands of spangles of pearlescent white. Marie watched them spiral earthward, entwining with the dancers in their descent.

When the shepherds and shepherdesses finished their dance, Nutcracker turned to Marie and asked, "Would you care to see some more of the magical kingdom?"

"Oh, yes, please!" came the reply.

Without a word, Nutcracker clapped his hands once, and a

large swan appeared, with feathers of the softest, whitest down. The swan dipped her elegant wings to enable Marie and Nutcracker to climb onto her back, and then glided swiftly over the brilliant landscape. Before long, Marie spied a fantastic vision in the distance. Through the swirling clouds rose up a rose-tinged palace surrounded by exquisitely filigreed gates (which immediately swung open upon their arrival), fashioned entirely from spun sugar, as delicate as cotton candy.

The castle's pastel walls, which, Nutcracker explained, were made of marzipan, glistened with candied fruits and peppermint drops, and its myriad towers appeared to have been constructed of marshmallow and meringue. Jewels of rock candy sparkled from the parapets, and the whole creation was surrounded by a moat of rose water. Here it was that their graceful chariot came to a stop.

As Marie and Nutcracker passed through the gateway, a troop of silver soldiers saluted them. "Welcome to the Palace of the Sugar Plums!" Nutcracker said. "Welcome! Welcome!" the soldiers echoed.

A wide staircase spread before them, and at its summit stood quite the most exquisite lady Marie had ever seen. She was dressed

entirely in a gown of silvery white. A glittering crown adorned her dainty head, and her entire being seemed suffused with a sweet luster. Nutcracker introduced this delicate creature to Marie as the Sugar Plum Fairy. The Sugar Plum Fairy smiled and curtsied, and waved her hand toward the delights that awaited them.

"May I present Mademoiselle Marie Stahlbaum?" said Nutcracker. "She is the one who saved my life! If she hadn't thrown her slipper just in the nick of time, I would be lying in a cold grave at this moment, bitten to death by the evil Mouse King!"

As Marie and Nutcracker ascended the stairs, they perceived a great ballroom, and many guests, all dressed in wonderful finery. At the Sugar Plum Fairy's request, Nutcracker described his battle with the Mouse King, and related how Marie had rescued him from his enchantment.

All of the assembled guests embraced Marie and praised her in unison: "Oh, you noble savior of our beloved prince! Dear, dear Marie!"

They then led Marie and Nutcracker into a hall of the castle where the walls shone with sparkling crystal. The furniture charmed Marie. There were the loveliest chairs, bureaus, and din-

ing tables, all made of cedar or brazilwood, and all covered with golden flowers.

The Sugar Plum Fairy bade Marie and Nutcracker sit down while a feast was brought before them: teas, cakes and the rarest of fruits. The food was a feast, first for the eyes, then for the palate. As Marie and Nutcracker found themselves famished after their travels, they devoured every morsel. While they ate, the courtiers of the Kingdom of Sugar Plums executed some clever diversions designed to beguile their guests.

To the click of castanets, ladies with flashing dark eyes and scarlet dresses curled sinuously in a dance of Spain. To Marie's enchantment, the dancers stomped their feet and swirled their costumes around her, before disappearing in a blaze of ruffles.

Marie hardly had time to nibble at her sweetmeats before the next diversion was presented: the music abruptly changed to an adagio tempo. Arabian dancers dressed in gauzy veils garnished with gold medallions and jewels swayed hypnotically past. Their feet, shod in curled-toe slippers, seemed borne on magic carpets, and the rich aroma of coffee drifted past.

"So many wonderful dancers!" Marie cried. "Each one is

more exciting than the last."

Nutcracker pointed toward the doors, as an enormous china teapot rolled into the room on little golden wheels. The shrill notes of a reed flute startled Marie and Nutcracker. A score of Chinese acrobats popped out of the pot dressed in gay satin jackets and trousers of every hue. This energetic troupe juggled plates and jumped through hoops, all the while springing merry somersaults all around the banquet hall, on the tables, and over the guests' heads.

Marie squealed with pleasure as, one by one, the dancers vaulted back into their teapot. Three more powerful dancers pushed the teapot away. These dancers were dressed as Russian peasants, in white shirts, black pantaloons, boots and brightly colored cummerbunds. Towering furry hats sat on their heads; Marie wondered why the hats didn't fall off with all the jumping and dancing about. Booming music filled the banquet hall, and the three dancers whirled faster and faster, until Marie could barely see their feet. They made great leaps and high kicks, shouting encouragement to one another as they did so. Marie had never seen anything so thrilling. With a final whoop of exuberance and a grand flourish, the men finished their dance and sprang from the hall, their boots hardly touching the floor.

Several moments passed before Marie became aware of a swishing and rustling nearby. At first, she was alarmed, anxious that the Mouse King might somehow have returned to seek revenge. However, Nutcracker touched her arm and assured her that all was well.

Then, a giggling and tittering arose among the guests.

"Shh! It's Madame Mirliton! Auntie Bonbon!"

In she swept, seven feet tall, and seven feet wide at the hips. All chirping and laughing, dozens of little candy-people scurried in and out of her gigantic hoop skirt, which swayed like a bell. Each time the bell swung, Marie caught glimpses of more candy people. How many could fit under there? The animated candies ran circles around their mistress's red-and-white striped legs, often bumping into one another. Auntie Bonbon sashayed over to Nutcracker and Marie, dropping an exaggerated curtsy. Nutcracker stood and bowed solemnly. He held out his hand to Marie, who returned Auntie Bonbon's curtsy. The candy-people broke into high-pitched peals of laughter. Shooing errant bonbons back under her skirt,

Auntie Bonbon clucked and reeled unsteadily out of the room.

Marie's sides hurt from laughing so much. Although she had partaken of many sweet delicacies, she felt merely pleasantly sated. Nutcracker smiled alongside her.

With a wave of her slender hand, the Sugar Plum Fairy summoned the next attraction. At once, the sparkling jeweled flowers slowly came to life and engaged in a waltz of sublime beauty and elegance. Oh, how they swayed in the invisible breeze! The first zephyrs of spring stirred the flowers' heads and imparted a sweet fragrance throughout the room. Their petals, composed of every pastel shade, appeared as fragile as angels' wings. They clustered together in bouquets, and then broke gently apart to form a continuous carpet of blooms. Marie could see every type of flower: full-blown roses, shy violets, sunny daisies, tender lilies, each weaving a gentle dance around the guests.

"Oh! How lovely!" Marie cried, clapping her hands as blossom by blossom, the flowers flitted away and the music subsided.

The Sugar Plum Fairy took several ladylike steps forward. One of her courtiers joined her as they began an elaborate dance of extreme delicacy. They floated through the air on celestial strains, their every movement a confection. How her dress floated about her like a cloud! How heavenly the music! Marie thought the dancers and music were the very essence of sweetness and light.

As they concluded their dance, all of the guests and dancers crowded into the hall around Nutcracker and Marie. The Sugar Plum Fairy placed a gentle kiss on Marie's forehead.

"You've all been so wonderful," Marie said, looking quickly from one face to another. Outside the castle windows, a glow appeared in the sky. Dawn approached.

Nutcracker held out his hand. Suddenly he seemed farther away, and separated from Marie by a haze.

"Stay, Marie . . . be my princess . . ."

"Nutcracker! Oh, Nutcracker!"

What was happening? The dancing figures all waved at Marie. It seemed to Marie as if what Nutcracker was saying was growing ever more indistinct. Presently she became aware that a silver mist was forming around her like a cloud. The dancers, the Sugar Plum Fairy, Nutcracker, and Marie herself were floating within it. A strange singing and buzzing and humming arose, then died away in the distance. Marie felt as if she were riding the crest

of a wave, climbing higher and higher-higher and higher-higher and . . .

Pum-poof! Marie fell from an unimaginable height. My, what a crash! When she opened her eyes, she was lying on the floor next to her own bed! It was broad daylight, and her mother was standing before her, saying, "Whatever happened to you, dearest Marie? You frightened us all out of our wits!"

Marie sat up and looked at the anxious faces that surrounded her.

"Oh, Mama, the most marvelous thing happened!"

Mama frowned. "Thank heaven I woke up in the middle of the night and wondered about you. When I came down the stairs I found you lying fast asleep under the Christmas tree, with all sorts of toys—Fritz's lead soldiers, stuffed animals, a jack-in-the-box—all around you. One of my best Christmas decorations was smashed to bits! And Nutcracker was lying by your feet, with your left slipper not far off!"

In earnest, Marie began to tell her mother of her wonderful adventures with Nutcracker, the Mouse King, and the fantastic Land of the Sugar Plums. Mama smoothed her hair back and kissed Marie.

"You have had a long, beautiful dream, Marie. But now you must put it all out of your head."

Marie insisted that she hadn't been dreaming at all. Before her mother could debate any further, the door to Marie's bedroom opened wide, and Uncle Drosselmeier stepped inside. He carried a parcel, and a twinkle was in his eye.

"Uncle Drosselmeier, how very naughty you were, to go up on top of the clock that way! Nutcracker needed your help!" Marie shouted.

Mama said, "Marie! Mind your manners!"

But Uncle Drosselmeier only smiled and handed the parcel to Marie.

"Don't be annoyed with me, little Marie, because I didn't destroy the Mouse King. After all, that was Nutcracker's job. How else could he have broken the enchantment? To make up for it, here's something that I know will make you happy."

Carefully, Marie undid the wrapping. She pulled out—Nutcracker! His teeth and broken jaw had been firmly fixed. Marie shouted for joy, and her mother laughed and said, "Now you see for yourself how nice Uncle Drosselmeier is to Nutcracker."

"Oh," murmured Marie, hugging him tightly, "If only you really were alive! I should love you forever!"

"But—" stammered Fritz, who'd heard voices and come into Marie's room, "How did Uncle Drosselmeier fix Nutcracker so quickly? How?"

Drosselmeier placed his hand on the boy's shoulder. "Things are not always as they appear, my boy." He guided Fritz to the door. Mama glanced quickly at Marie, completely absorbed in Nutcracker, and followed.

"Nutcracker! Oh, Nutcracker!" Marie sighed. "I shall love you forever! To me you are the handsomest prince in the whole world!" Once more she kissed her beloved Nutcracker, who smiled and winked.

Voices drifted up from the drawing room. "Marie! Marie! It's Christmas! Oh, do come downstairs and see what Uncle Drosselmeier has prepared for us!"

"Happy Christmas, Nutcracker, dear."

Marie picked up Nutcracker and went to join the others.

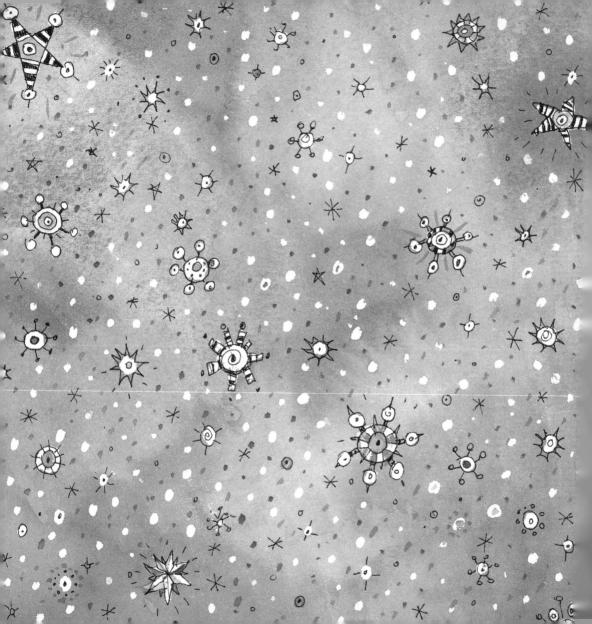